The Wild Baby
Gets a Puppy

Library of Congress Cataloging-in-Publication Data
Lindgren, Barbro.
The wild baby gets a puppy.
Translation of: Vilda bebin får en hund/by Barbro Lindgren.
Summary: Anxious to have a real puppy, Baby Ben is disappointed
when he gets a rag puppy for his birthday until he
discovers that "Rags" has some special qualities of his own.
[1. Dogs—Fiction.   2. Mothers and sons—Fiction.
3. Stories in rhyme]   I. Ericksson, Eva, ill.
II. Prelutsky, Jack.   III. Title.
PZ8.3.L616Wid 1988   [E]   87-212
ISBN 0-688-06711-5
ISBN 0-688-06712-3 (lib. bdg.)

Swedish text copyright © 1985 by Barbro Lindgren
Illustrations copyright © 1985 by Eva Eriksson
English text copyright © 1988 by Jack Prelutsky

The Wild Baby Gets a Puppy

by BARBRO LINDGREN

pictures by EVA ERIKSSON

adapted from the Swedish by

JACK PRELUTSKY

Greenwillow Books,

New York

"I want a puppy!" Ben announced,
"I've got to get one soon,"
he started nagging mama
one winter afternoon.

"If you won't give me one," he said,
"I'd like to have a horse instead,
  and if you think a horse won't do
  I'll take a cat, or maybe two."

But mama said, "I'm sorry dear,
no pets until your birthday's here."
Ben answered mama with a sigh,
"My birthday isn't till July.

"I cannot wait, I don't know how,
my birthday is too far from now."
But mama said, "My dearest Ben,
you'll simply have to wait till then."

Ben waited, till at last one day
his birthday was a day away,
he scarcely slept at all that night,
but tossed and tumbled left and right.

The sun finally rose, baby Ben was awake,
"Happy Birthday!" said mama,
"I've presents and cake."
One box was so big, that Ben happily cried,
"I wonder whatever is waiting inside."

He opened the lid,
and exclaimed with a squeal,
"There's a puppy in here,
but the puppy's not real.

"It's made out of rags, it can't run, it can't bark,
I can't ever take it for walks in the park.
Oh mama! I think that you've made a mistake."

"Don't be angry," said mama,
"have some of your cake."

Baby Ben ate his cake without even a smile,
deciding that he would stay angry awhile.

That night, as he lay sound asleep in his bed,
the puppy awakened, and lifted its head.

It soon began dancing and hopping around,
baby Ben heard the noise, and got up with a bound.

"My puppy is real!" he cried with delight.
"It looks like my birthday has turned out all right.
Just see how it prances, and how its tail wags,
it's a wonderful puppy, I'm naming it Rags."

His toys awoke to join the fun
when they heard all the fuss,
"Hooray, your puppy's real!" they said.
"Your puppy's one of us!"

Then baby Ben, and Bunny, too,
Giraffe, and even Mouse
climbed up upon the windowsill,
and leaped out of the house.

Rags was eager to explore,
and jumped out right behind the four.

They plunged into a water drum
and did not frown or fret,
"It's so much fun," said baby Ben,
"to be so soaking wet."

The air was warm,
they soon were dry,
they stood and watched
the sparkling sky.

Then Rags sprouted wings,
they hopped on his back,
clinging with all of their might,
baby Ben shouted "Fly!"
Rags answered, "Bow wow!"
and they rocketed into the night.

But as they flew, Mouse slipped and fell,
he waved and called, "Farewell! Farewell!"
"Oh no!" his friends began to bawl.
"Ho! Ho!" said Ben, "He likes to fall.
We'll fetch him when we turn around,
but now it's time to play,
and see as much as we can see,
so let's be on our way."

They landed on the Rabbit World,
and Bunny yelled "Hooray!"
He greeted all his cousins there,
"I'm visiting today!"

Giraffe looked down and laughed with glee,
"That planet's got giraffes like me."
He visited that friendly place
as baby Ben soared off through space.

Rags flew faster, Rags flew higher,
then lightning set Rags' tail afire.

Baby Ben was bold and bright,
and he did not delay,
he tugged that tail and took it off,
and tossed the flames away.

"Look! There's the moon," said baby Ben,
"why don't we go there now,
 I'd like to see who lives on it."
And Rags replied, "Bow wow!"

They flew and flew, and very soon
the pair alit upon the moon.
Lots of puppies frolicked there,
and babies too—no room to spare.

Ben exclaimed, "There's so much noise!
So many busy girls and boys.
The moon is much too full today,
I think I'd better go away."

They flew and flew, until they found
the Ice Cream Planet, flat and round,
and gulping ice cream sweet and cold,
they ate as much as they could hold.

They stuffed themselves without a care,
then drifted downward through the air.

Soon Bunny and Giraffe and Mouse
fell gently by their side,
and everyone had peaceful smiles,
and all were sleepy-eyed.

Ben landed softly on the ground,
happy, weary, safe and sound.

When Ben took Rags outside next day
Mama shook her head,
she stared at them in disbelief,
"Oh my!" was all she said.

BARBRO LINDGREN is the author of *The Wild Baby* (an *SLJ* Best Book of 1981) and *The Wild Baby Goes to Sea* (an *SLJ* Best Book of 1983), and of the popular toddler series of books about Sam. She lives in Sweden.

EVA ERIKSSON is familiar to young readers as the illustrator of the Wild Baby books and of the Sam series. She is also the illustrator of Rose and Samuel Lagercrantz's *Brave Little Pete of Geranium Street*, which was adapted from the Swedish by Jack Prelutsky. She lives in Sweden.

JACK PRELUTSKY has written more than 30 books, including *The New Kid on the Block, The Queen of Eene, The Snopp on the Sidewalk,* and *Nightmares* (all ALA Notable Books), and *Ride a Purple Pelican.* He also adapted *The Wild Baby* and *The Wild Baby Goes to Sea* from the Swedish. Born and raised in New York, he and his wife now live in Albuquerque, New Mexico.